This igloo book belongs to:

....

igloobooks

Published in 2019
by Igloo Books Ltd
Cottage Farm
Sywell
NN6 0BJ
www.igloobooks.com

Copyright © 2013 Igloo Books Ltd
Igloo Books is an imprint of Bonnier Books UK

1219 003
6 8 10 11 9 7 5
ISBN 978-1-78197-469-8

Written by Carrie Lewis
Illustrated by Christopher Embleton

Printed and manufactured in China

YOU'RE A CHEEKY MONKEY

igloobooks

It was early morning in the jungle. The sleepy monkeys snored and snoozed and dozed and dreamed, but Cheeky Monkey was wide awake and he wanted to play!

Mummy's tail dangled in front of Cheeky Monkey's nose.
"Wake up, Mummy," he said, giggling and tugging it.
"You cheeky little monkey!" she cried.

Cheeky Monkey swung through the trees. Soon, he spotted Parrot sleeping. Cheeky Monkey grinned. "BOO!" he yelled, jumping out at Parrot.

"SQUAWK, SQUAWK, SCREEEECH!" went Parrot, flying away in fright. The noise woke all the other animals up. They covered their ears in horror.

Next, Cheeky Monkey snuck up on Snake in the tall, green grass. "Got you!" he cried, jumping out and tickling Snake all over.

"HEE, HEE, HEE!" laughed Snake. He wriggled and jiggled and giggled, until he got all tied up in a great big knot.

In the river, Hippo and Crocodile were just about to eat their lunch. Cheeky Monkey swung past with a **WHOOSH**, grabbing Hippo's tasty banana.

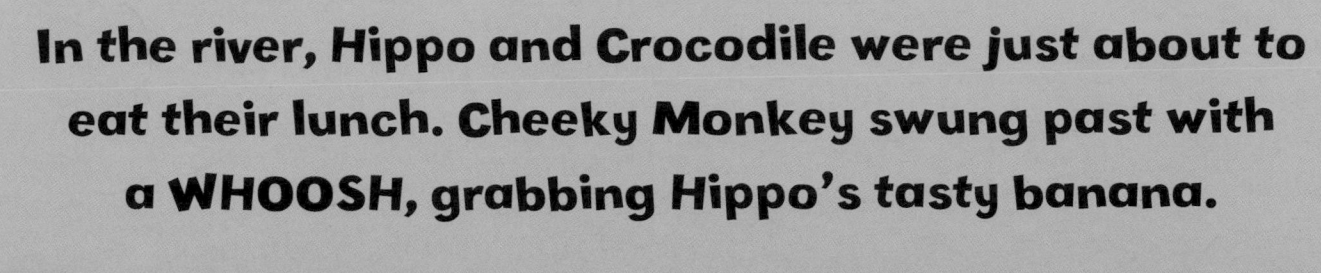

Hippo and Crocodile grumbled and mumbled as Cheeky Monkey took a big, chompy bite out of the banana and plopped the skin back down on Crocodile's head.

At the waterfall, Cheeky Monkey saw Elephant having a lovely, slurpy drink. "I'll dress up as a monster and give him a fright," thought Cheeky Monkey, giggling.

"Oo-oo!" went Cheeky Monkey and he leapt out of the bushes. "Aargh!" cried Elephant in surprise, spraying water all over the jungle with a SPLASH.

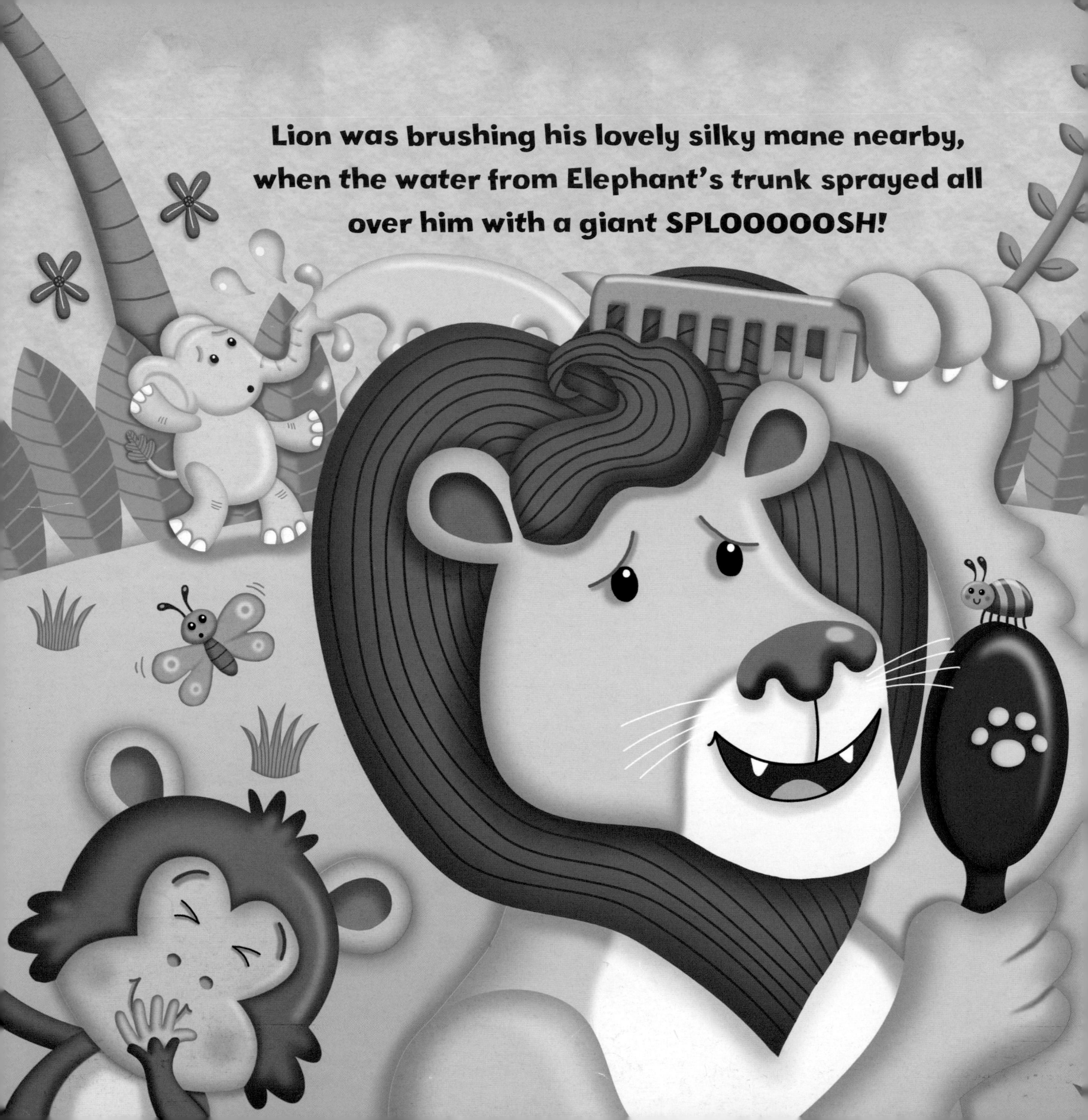

Lion was brushing his lovely silky mane nearby, when the water from Elephant's trunk sprayed all over him with a giant SPLOOOOOSH!

Lion was soaked from head to toe and his stylish mane was ruined. "GRRRR!" Lion growled. Cheeky Monkey thought it was very funny. He ran off into the jungle, giggling.

"I've had enough of that Cheeky Monkey!" thought Lion.
"It's time something was done about him." He gathered all the
animals together for a meeting.

"Cheeky Monkey is just too cheeky," said Lion to the other animals. "I think **WE** should play our own trick and give **HIM** a big surprise."

Elephant hid behind a tree, Crocodile and Snake hid amongst the leaves and Parrot pretended to be a flower. Hippo blew bubbles from underwater and the monkeys all giggled.

"SHHHH! Everybody BE QUIET!" growled Lion from behind a log. "Here comes Cheeky Monkey."

Cheeky Monkey came swinging through the trees
but he couldn't find the monkeys, Parrot, Snake, Hippo,
Crocodile, Elephant, or even Lion. Where had everyone gone?

Cheeky Monkey didn't giggle then. Where were all his friends and family? It was no fun being all alone in the jungle.

Suddenly, there was a rustling and a flapping and a wriggling and all the animals jumped out of their hiding places.
"BOOOOO!"

"We got you, Cheeky Monkey!" they all said, laughing.
"I'm sorry I played tricks," he replied. "I won't do it again."

"You're a very cheeky monkey, but we can be cheeky, too!"
said the animals, giggling! After that, everyone played
happily together and Cheeky Monkey was a very
happy monkey, indeed.